For Ollie, Alice and Lexie S.P-H.

For Theodore, my little digger expert! E.E.

An Imprint of Sterling Publishing
1166 Avenue of The Americas
New York, NY, 10036

SANDY CREEK and the distinctive Sandy Creek logo
are registered trademarks of Barnes & Noble, Inc.

Text © 2015 by Smriti Prasadam-Halls
Illustrations © 2015 by Ed Eaves

This 2016 edition published by Sandy Creek.

ISBN 978-1-4351-6334-8

Manufactured in China
Lot #:

2 4 6 8 10 9 7 5 3 1
04/16

Ready, Set, DIG!

Smriti Prasadam-Halls   Ed Eaves

Let's go to work, Construction Crew!
Time to see what you can do.
Put your toughness to the test,
Build, build, build your very best.

Motors starting, **BRMM BRMM BRMM!**
Engines revving, **VRMM VRMM VRMM!**

Get in gear, don't be slow!
Ready, set... **OFF WE GO!**

CONNOR CRANE is at the ready,
With his steel chain holding steady.

High up hanging,
CLINGING, CLANGING.

His wrecking ball goes BASH, BASH, BASH!
Ready, set...
SMASH, SMASH, CRASH!

DUMPER DAVE is big and tough,
For any job, he's strong enough.
CREEPING, CRAWLING,
HEAVING,
HAULING.

MIXER MILLIE spins and hums,
Cement is churning in her drum.

BARREL WHIRLING,
CONCRETE SWIRLING.

Spread it thick to build and fix,
Ready, set...

MIX, MIX,
MIX!

RAVI ROLLER takes his spot,
Squashing asphalt, wet and hot.

SQUELCHING,

SPLATTERING,

SQUEEZING,

FLATTENING.

Press it smooth, no bumps or holes,
Ready, set…

ROLL, ROLL, ROLL!

DOUG THE DIGGER

loves to dig,
Gobbling earth,
however big.

MUNCHING, CRUNCHING,
SCRAPING, SCRUNCHING.

...OOPS!

Oh dear, oh dear, what bad luck,
Doug the Digger's

STUCK, STUCK, STUCK!

He gives a **YELL,**
he gives a **SHOUT,**
Can anybody get him out?

ALL his friends roar into action,
Wheels a-turning, gaining traction.

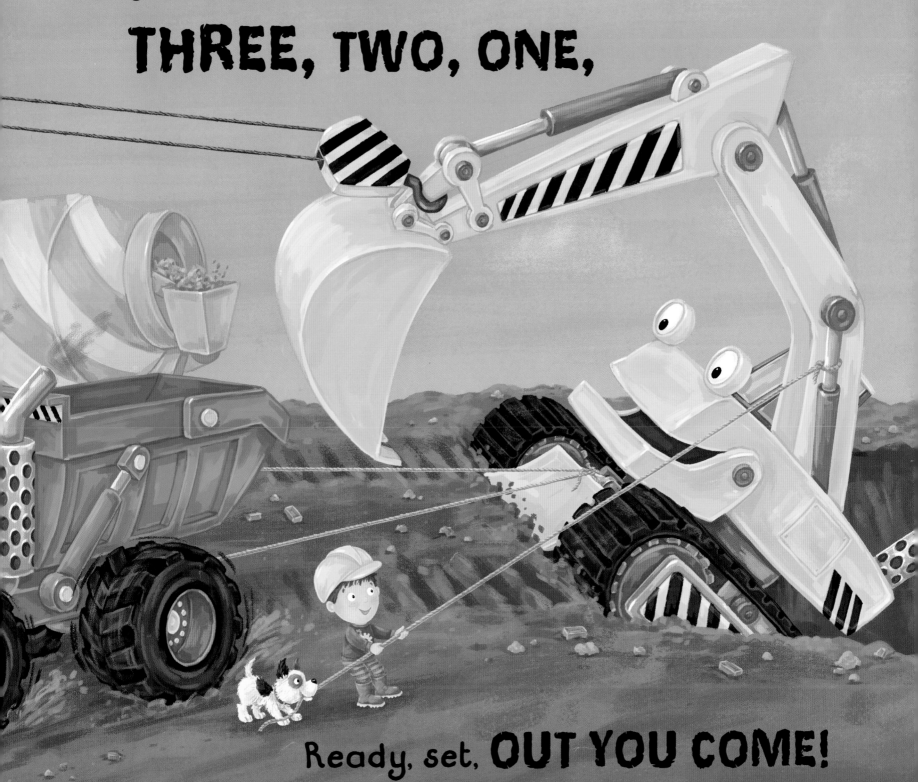

Hang in there, Doug!
THREE, TWO, ONE,

Ready, set, OUT YOU COME!

WELL DONE, TEAM! All safely back!
Now let's keep going, stay on track.
Complete the project, brick by brick,
And get the job done,
DOUBLE QUICK.

Shunting, shifting,
loading, lifting,

Using all your strength and skill.
READY, SET...

Construction Crew, you've done your best.
Construction Crew, it's time to rest.
So no more rushing,
Just hush, hush, hushing.

Not another HONK or BEEP...

READY, SET...
time to SLEEP! sssss

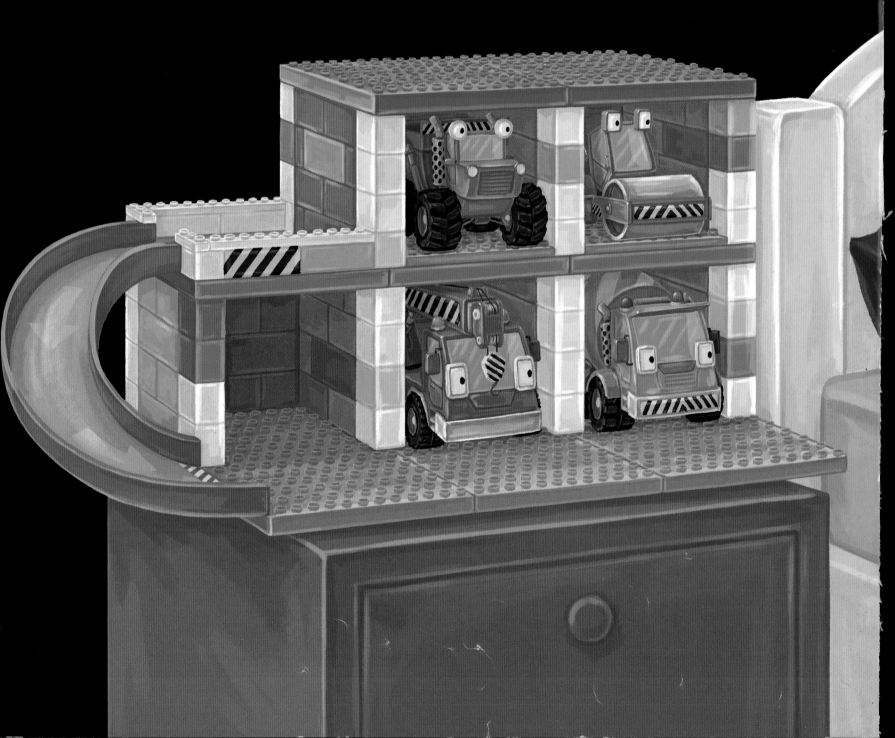